DO YOU ENJOY BEING FRIGHTENED?

**WOULD YOU RATHER HAVE
NIGHTMARES
INSTEAD OF SWEET DREAMS?**

**ARE YOU HAPPY ONLY WHEN
SHAKING WITH FEAR?**

CONGRATULATIONS ! ! ! !

YOU'VE MADE A WISE CHOICE.

**THIS BOOK IS THE DOORWAY
TO ALL THAT MAY FRIGHTEN YOU.**

GET READY FOR

**COLD, CLAMMY SHIVERS
RUNNING UP AND DOWN YOUR SPINE!**

NOW, OPE
IF YOU

Shivers

THE GHOST WRITER

M. D. Spenser

Paradise Press, Inc.

Plantation, Florida

To John and Daniel

Published by Paradise Press, Inc. by arrangement with River Publishing, Inc. All right, title and interest to the "SHIVERS" logo and design are owned by River Publishing, Inc. No portion of the "SHIVERS" logo and design may be reproduced in part or whole without prior written permission from River Publishing, Inc. An application for a registered trademark of the "SHIVERS" logo and design is pending with the Federal Patent and Trademark office.

ISBN 1-57657-053-3

EXCLUSIVE DISTRIBUTION BY PARADISE PRESS, INC.

Cover Design by George Paturzo
Cover Illustration by Eddie Roseboom

Printed in the U.S.A.
30631

Chapter One

Amber Elliston loved her life. But she hated a lot of things, too. Asparagus. The gross smell when her dad smoked his pipe. The dumb dress with a big bow on it that her mom made her wear to a wedding.

But so far in her twelve years, she had hated nothing more than this.

Her family was moving.

They were going to live in some lame small town in Georgia where nothing ever happened. So what if her mom, Carol, had grown up in Jackson? Big deal. That didn't mean she had to live there again.

This place didn't have a movie theater. There wasn't an FAO Schwarz. Or even a McDonald's!

Boring, boring, boring. Amber thought to herself. My life is over.

How was she supposed to know about the strange and scary secret that was waiting for her in Jackson? The one that would change her life forever?

It was August. The Elliston family sat crammed into their black Honda, driving away from Amber's home.

Ever since she was a baby, she, her older brother, David, and her parents had lived in an apartment in a tall building in New York City.

Amber loved it there. She loved the rows of skyscrapers out her window high above the busy street. She loved running to the elevator in the lobby, and pushing the button that said UP. She would miss the noise outside. She already missed playing in the crowded park. She missed her friends.

"You can write to them," her mother said, trying to make Amber feel better.

"Write them? Nobody writes letters anymore," Amber complained. She knew she would probably never see her home again.

Amber looked out the window of the back seat for a long time. She watched her city disappear. As the family drove south, the towns got smaller and smaller. Finally, they were in a hot, lonely part of the country where there were more trees and fields than houses.

David rode in the back seat, too. He spent most of the time reading a book. It was one of those adventure stories about dragons and castles that boys seemed to like. He was fourteen, and didn't talk much anymore. His legs had gotten so long he had to stick his knees up just to fit in the car.

Amber's mom sat in the front looking at a map. Her dad was driving.

Amber looked at the back of her dad's head and was angry. He was the reason they were doing this. It had all started when her dad was walking home from work late one night. That was when he had felt a cold, clammy hand on his shoulder.

And a gun pressed hard against his back.

Chapter Two

Amber's dad had decided to move the day he got mugged.

He had lived in New York all his life, but no one had ever tried to hurt him like that before. Thankfully, a police officer had walked by just as the big, scary man pulled the gun. The thief ran off into the night. And Amber's dad wasn't hurt.

But it changed his life forever.

Other than being her dad, he was Mark Elliston, Newspaper Editor. After years of working for The New York Times, he had suddenly decided to take a new job. He was going to own the newspaper in the small town where her mom was from.

Amber would never forget the day he told them.

"Guess what? I've got great news," her dad said with a smile that looked fake.

He ran his fingers through his long shaggy hair

like he always did when he was nervous. She and David sat on the sofa waiting for the worst.

"I'm tired of living in the city," Dad said. "We're moving to Georgia."

"Georgia!" Amber and David said in disbelief. "Where is that?"

Amber started crying. David went to his room and slammed the door.

"Oh come on," Dad said. "You're going to like it. Really. I promise. There's too much crime here in the city. This is a chance for us to spend more time together. Everything is going to be okay."

Sure, Amber thought. Everything's going to be okay. For *you*. It's always about you, she thought. What about us?

For days, Amber and David begged not to go. They had long talks with their mother.

"Why? Why do we have to do this?" Amber pleaded. "I'm not moving!"

"Honey, it will all be for the best. You'll see," her mom said. "I can still do my job, and I think your dad will be much happier."

Amber's mom was a graphic artist. That meant she drew pictures on a computer, which she could do anywhere. She sold them to people, who put them on things like brochures and greeting cards. One time she even made a picture that they used on MTV in between videos. That was pretty cool.

But Georgia? Way uncool.

Amber went on strike and refused to come out of her room for hours. Or at least until she got hungry. David put a note on his door that said "Parent Free Zone." He played Myst for a whole week.

But that didn't change a thing. Here they were on their way to Jackson, Georgia. Wherever that was.

The Elliston family had been in the car for fourteen hours. Amber curled up on her pillow, which was the last thing she took from her room before the movers came. She felt like someone was dragging her away. Or pulling her away. She closed her eyes and listened to the road hum underneath the tires.

A song came on the radio. It wasn't anything she usually listened to, like rap or rock. Or that boring public radio her mom always had on. It was a really old tune. There was a piano playing. It sounded like the music from one of those old films her mom watched all the time on cable. It reminded Amber of the movie with a pretty woman who sang into one of those standup microphones. A high, haunting voice began a song.

"Come to me, come to me, oh beautiful one. Come to me, or I shall come to you . . . "

The sad melody made Amber look out the window. It was night now, and very black. There were no lights anywhere. It was so dark all she could see was the faint outline of her own reflection in the window.

Amber stared at it like she was looking in a mirror. Slowly, something started to change in the glass. Her long straight brown hair drew up and became light and curly. There was a flower tucked in her hair over her ear. Her lips curled up into a big smile with bright red lipstick. She laughed.

But Amber had not moved her own face at all.

Then she saw it. The painted mouth slowly whispered.

"Come to me, come to me, oh beautiful one. Come to me, or I shall come to you."

Amber's eyes opened wide. She put her hand over her mouth.

Suddenly, the face in the window became very frightened. Its eyes got big, and started to cry. It screwed up into a horrifying ball of terror and pain.

Suddenly, there was a terrible scream.

Chapter Three

"Honey! Honey! Are you okay?"

It was Amber's mom. She was leaning over the back seat, shaking her daughter's leg.

"Jeez, you scared me to death," David said. "What's your problem? You sounded like you'd seen a ghost or something."

"I did! I did see something!" Amber insisted. "It was a face. And it was looking at me in the window!"

"Oh, Amber. You must have had a bad dream," Mom said.

"Or maybe something popped out at you. A Velociraptor maybe. Eeeek! Eeeek!" David teased. He leaned over and pretended to bite her arm.

"Stop it! Stop it!" Amber cried. She hated that dinosaur movie, especially the part where the girl had to hide in the kitchen. That's what she felt like now.

Trapped and afraid. Something weird had happened. Something unnatural. She had seen that face. It was real!

Or maybe she really had just fallen asleep.

"Honey, it's okay. It's been a long day and I'm sure you're tired," Mom said in her comforting voice. "Settle down. It's time to wake up now. We're getting close."

"Close to nothing," David grumbled.

Their car hummed along a narrow country road. Rain started falling. Amber's dad turned on the windshield wipers. The drops got bigger, so he made the wipers go even faster. Soon the rain got so hard that Amber couldn't see out the front window. Even the light from the car headlights could barely shine through the huge sheets of rain that pounded through the darkness. The downpour was so loud it sounded like water gushing from the fire hydrants on her street back in New York.

"Here," Mom said, pointing to the left. "I think we turn here."

Amber's dad slowed down the car, and turned onto a dark narrow road. Amber heard a ping-ping-ping noise under the car. Her mom explained that it was gravel. They didn't have paved streets out here.

9

The road went deep into the woods. Her dad drove very slowly now. Amber could tell he was nervous. He gripped the steering wheel tightly with both hands. Mom was leaning forward in her seat, trying to see through the pounding rain and the black night.

As they wound around curve after curve, the headlights hit things Amber had never seen before. A yellow sign blew wildly in the wind. It had a picture of a cow on it.

What was that all about, she wondered?

Around another curve, the headlights lit up a rusty old car half way down a ditch. She saw a big black mailbox. Then the car headed over a wooden, one lane bridge. The water underneath sounded like the roar of a subway train.

Suddenly lightning flashed, lighting up their faces as if they were having their picture taken. Bang! The thunder cracked right on top of their car!

"I'm scared!" Amber cried as the wind blew against the Honda.

Then Mom screamed.

"Mark! Look out! Someone's in the road!"

The last thing Amber remembered seeing was the flash of a young girl in the headlights. She was wearing an old white party dress and standing right in front of a giant tree next to the river bank.

Their Honda was heading straight for her, until Amber's dad swerved. She heard the sound of the tires skidding on the gravel. Amber clutched her seat belt right before she heard the loud *BOOM!* followed by the tinkling of broken glass.

She felt something wrap itself around her neck.

Chapter Four

Amber looked up from the back seat of the car. A giant tree limb had crashed through the front windshield. Its branches stuck into their car like legs from a giant wooden spider. Sticks and twigs were strewn all over the place — in her hair, all over her clothes. A vine was wrapped around her neck.

She looked over at David, who was brushing leaves off his wet shirt.

"Oh my gosh! Oh my gosh! Is everyone all right?"

It was her dad's voice.

"Yes, yes, I'm okay," Amber's mom answered. "Kids! Are you all right?"

"Yeah, I'm okay," David said.

Amber couldn't speak. She just cried.

"Boy, that was a scare," Dad said. "Let's not panic. First, everyone make sure they're not hurt in any way. Can you move? Do you hurt anywhere?"

The family sat in silence for several minutes. All of a sudden, the rain stopped. They heard the sound of a car up ahead. Amber could see the head-lights coming towards them.

"Hey, is anybody in there?" a man's voice shouted. They heard the slam of a car door.

Amber's dad managed to open the door on his side of the Honda. He got out, shaky, but okay.

"Hello! Yes, I think we're all fine here," he said to the man. "Couldn't see in all this rain, and I guess we got too far off the road."

"Well, you're really lucky. You almost hit that big tree there," the man said. "Good thing you swerved in time to run into nothing but that branch. I'm Bill Johnson. I'm the sheriff around these parts. What are you doing out here this time of night?"

"We're the Ellistons," Amber's dad said. "We're moving here. I guess that makes us your new neighbors."

"Oh yeah," the man said, running his hand over his gray beard. "I know about you. You're the ones who bought the old McAfee place. You're from New York, aren't you?"

"Yes," Amber's mom said. By this time she

had gotten out of the car too. "I'm Carol Elliston. Actually, I used to be Carol McAfee. That's my grandmother's old house. It's been empty for years, but we decided to buy it and fix it up. I lived in Jackson when I was a little girl, but we moved to the city a long time ago. I haven't been back here since then. Mark's going to be the new editor down at the paper."

Amber's dad suddenly asked, "What was that young girl doing out here in the middle of the night? She was standing in front of that tree. We nearly hit her!"

Mr. Johnson stared at them for a long time. When he spoke again, he did not mention the girl.

Chapter Five

"Well, tell you what," Sheriff Johnson said finally. "Doesn't look like your car is going to be getting anywhere for a while. What do you say we get everybody in my patrol car and let's get you home."

Their parents turned and looked at Amber and David and motioned for them to get out of the car. It wasn't easy, but Amber crawled over the mess and climbed out on David's side.

Everyone piled into Sheriff Johnson's big yellow and black Ford. It had a radio in the front, pieces of paper all over the floor and Coke cans scattered about.

"Wait a minute!" Amber called out.

She hopped out of the car, ran back to the Honda and grabbed her pillow.

"Guess you'll need that tonight, honey," her mom said. "We all could use some sleep."

Sheriff Johnson drove up the road, around a

curve, and started up a hill. They saw a small farm-house. They passed a wide open space, then another house. Then a barn, then one more house. All the buildings looked very old, and were made out of wood.

The patrol car turned left and headed up a steep hill. Amber figured this must be a driveway.

"Well, here you are," Sheriff Johnson said, pulling the car to a stop.

Everyone got out and stood and stared at their new home. The house was much bigger than Amber had expected. Although it was night, a full moon had popped from behind the clouds so Amber could see clearly.

The house was three stories high, with big pointed windows sticking up on top. There was a long porch that wrapped all the way around the front. An empty rocking chair creaked back and forth.

Must be the wind, Amber thought.

"Wow, you weren't kidding when you said this place needed fixing up," Dad said to Amber's mom.

"Well, honey, no one has lived here in fifty years," Mom said sheepishly. She had only shown Dad pictures of the place, taken when she was a kid. "I think a little paint and elbow grease will do the job."

Sheriff Johnson was very quiet.

"Nope," he said. "I don't think anybody has lived here since the accident."

Chapter Six

The accident? Amber thought.

Her mom and dad stared silently at each other.

"I think it's about time we got in out of this weather and got some sleep," Dad said finally, changing the subject. "Amber, why don't you be the first to walk through the door of our new home?"

He tried to make it sound as if it was a big honor.

"The real estate lady told me there's no lock on the door," Mom said. "You can probably walk right in."

Amber climbed slowly up the front steps. Her sandals made creaky noises as she walked across the wooden boards of the porch.

She came to a giant door, with all kinds of fancy swirls around the edges. A big M was carved in the middle. A metal door knocker dangled from a single nail, and looked as if it was about to fall off.

Amber reached out and touched the door knob. It was funny looking — made of some kind of white glass that was very cold when she touched it.

Slowly, she turned the knob. Just as she was about to push the door inward, something pulled hard on the other side. It jerked her so quickly she fell face down inside, onto a very cold, hard floor.

A creepy glowing light hit her straight in the face.

Chapter Seven

"Gotcha!"

Amber heard a scary — but very familiar — laugh.

"David! I hate you!" she cried.

She looked up to see her brother standing inside the house in front of her, holding a flashlight.

"Oooooo. Ooooooo-oooo! I'm the ghost of the old house! I'm the face you saw through the car window," he said. "I'm coming to get you."

He held the flashlight up under his chin, making his face glow like a monster's.

"David, you come out here this instant," Mom said in her I'm-really-angry-now voice. "That was a really mean trick to play on your sister."

"Oh, Mom. I was just kidding," he said, hoping he wouldn't get into trouble.

"How did you get in there?" Dad asked.

"While you were talking, I went around to the back. The door there was wide open, so I just came on in," he said. "Boy, this place is a mess!"

Mom had had enough.

"Look, we've been through a lot tonight," she said. "It's getting really late. Let's all go inside and let Sheriff Johnson go home."

David pointed the flashlight into the big living room. A huge fireplace was built into one wall. Paint peeled from the ceiling.

Amber's dad took the flashlight from David and shone it around the room. It finally lit up a long string hanging down from a light bulb.

"Here, this should do the trick," he said, pulling on the cord.

A bare light flashed on. Now they could see the room around them.

It was completely empty.

"Drat!" Mom said. "The furniture isn't here yet! The moving company told me they were going to deliver everything today!"

"Oh, honey. Don't worry," Amber's dad said. "They probably got stuck in all this rain."

"I've got some blankets and sleeping bags out in the patrol car," Sheriff Johnson said. "You can use those tonight."

Amber's dad followed him outside.

David started walking through the old house, turning on lights like he had seen his father do. There was a big bedroom off to one side.

"This is where your dad and I are going to sleep," Mom said.

As Amber and her mom looked at the big, dusty room, they heard a loud crash.

"Mom! Mom!" David shouted from the next room. "Something's got a hold of my foot!"

Chapter Eight

Amber and her mom ran to where David was screaming.

He was lying on a big, winding staircase. It led up to a dark hallway on the second floor of the house. His foot was sticking down inside one of the steps.

The old wood had cracked underneath David's big tennis shoes. His foot had gone straight through the step.

"David, David," Mom said reassuringly. "Nothing's got your foot except that old step. Look down and you'll see. You've fallen in through a hole in the wood."

David looked down and pulled his foot out of the broken step. He looked embarrassed that the accident had scared him so much.

"Guess we'll have to get some carpenters in to fix that as soon as possible," Mom said. "Especially since your bedrooms are upstairs. Let's go up and take a look."

The three of them climbed the rickety steps to the second floor. Another bedroom opened to their right. On their left, they found a smaller room with a big window.

"This is where you're going to sleep, Amber," Mom said. "This is your new room."

Amber wasn't sure she liked it very much. It was musty, and smelled like the closed-up section of the library at her old school. But the window was really neat. It was taller than any she had ever seen before in someone's house. And there was a seat built right into it!

I could sit there and read my books, she thought. Or talk on the phone to my friends.

Then she got sad. She remembered that she didn't have any friends to talk to here. But she was too tired to think too much about that now.

She yawned.

Dad and Sheriff Johnson walked into the room with a bundle of sleeping bags.

"Here you go," Dad said. "This should get us through the night."

Amber's mom helped her spread the soft blankets over the hard floor. Amber still clutched her pillow. She plopped down on her makeshift bed, holding the pillow close to her chest.

"Goodnight," Mom said, rubbing Amber's hair softly. It made her feel safe, like when she was a little girl back in New York. "Everything will be better in the morning," Mom added. "You'll see."

Amber lay on the floor a long time, but could not go to sleep. The moon was bright. She almost felt as if she was back in the city, where the lights outside never went out.

She could see her room clearly now. There were big flowers on the wallpaper. An empty bookshelf was built into a closet. Someone had left an old picture of the ocean on the wall.

I'll have to get rid of that, Amber thought. Right then she decided one of the first things she would do when the movers came would be to put up her posters.

And I could hang my crystals in this big window, she thought excitedly.

She jumped up and ran over to see just where they could go.

Looking outside, she noticed that her house sat at the top of a big hill. The moon lit up the yard, which rolled steeply down toward a house next door.

Funny, she hadn't noticed it when they drove in.

It was much smaller than Amber's home. She could barely see what it looked like, except for a light in a window upstairs.

Wow! Someone must live there! Amber thought. Maybe it was a family. A family with kids! Maybe there was a girl she could play with. That would be great!

Amber pressed her face to the glass to get a better look. Suddenly, she saw a shadow behind the curtains of the other house. It was the outline of a person, but Amber could not tell whether it was a boy or girl.

She wiped the dust off her window and stared harder.

Suddenly, the curtains moved. Someone was standing in the other window!

It was not a kid. It was an old lady with long white hair that hung to her waist. She had very white skin, and coal black eyes that shone in the dark.

And they were staring straight at Amber!

<u>Chapter Nine</u>

The next thing Amber knew, it was morning. The sun was filtering down on her face. It was hot and sticky.

Then she remembered. She wasn't in her bed in New York. She was on the floor of a spooky old house that was going to be her home now. No bed. No friends. Not even any air conditioning.

Amber lay on the strange blankets and looked at the ceiling. Then she sat straight up.

That lady! That lady was staring at me from the window last night! She remembered. Suddenly she was afraid.

Amber jumped up off the floor, and ran into the hall and down the stairs.

"Mom! Mom!" she cried.

She heard the sounds of someone cooking. The smell of bacon hung in the air. But where was the kitchen in this old house? Where was her family?

"Honey, I'm in here. In the back of the house," Mom's familiar voice said. "Just keep going straight ahead of you."

Amber walked toward the back of the house and into the huge, old kitchen. Her mom stood over a big, white stove. She was poking at something in a big black skillet.

"Feel like some breakfast?" Mom asked with a smile.

"Sure, I guess so," Amber said. "But where did you get any food? Or stuff to cook with? Have the movers come?"

"No, not yet. But Sheriff Johnson came over first thing this morning and brought up a whole box of supplies. And some pots and pans to make things in. His wife sent over bacon, eggs and even some home-made biscuits. Come on over here and get yourself a plate. You're about to sample some real country cooking."

Suddenly, Amber didn't feel like eating.

"Mom," she said. "I saw something really scary last night."

"We all saw some pretty scary things last night, honey," Mom said. "But Sheriff Johnson, Daddy and David have gone to get the Honda. They think it will be okay as soon as we get the windshield fixed. And the movers will probably show up today with all our things. I promise — it's going to start feeling just like home, real soon."

"But that's not what I'm talking about," Amber said. "I saw something outside my window last night."

"What?" Mom asked.

"Well, after I went to bed I couldn't sleep. So I got up and looked outside," Amber said. "Did you know there's a house just down that hill?"

"Yes," Mom nodded. "It's been there for a very long time."

"But Mom," Amber continued. "When I looked over at it last night, there was someone in the window. It was an old lady. And she looked just like a witch!"

Chapter Ten

Amber's mom turned off the stove and set the food aside.

"Sit down," she said. "I want to tell you something."

The two of them sat cross-legged in the middle of the empty floor.

"That was not a witch you saw," Mom explained. "That's old Miss McAfee. She's lived here all her life. In fact, she used to live in this house when she was a little girl. And she's related to you. She's your great aunt. That means she was your grandmother's sister."

This was all very confusing. Amber had never known her grandmother. She had died before Amber was born. In fact, she didn't know any of her mother's family. They had never been to New York. And Amber's family had never been here.

Before now.

"Remember last night when Sheriff Johnson said no one had lived in this house since the accident?" Mom asked.

"Yes," Amber said. "But I didn't know what he was talking about."

"Well, many years ago, the whole McAfee family lived in this house. There were three sisters — Helen, Hannah and Harriet. Harriet was my mother — your grandmother. Helen and Hannah were my aunts. That would make them your great aunts. The woman you saw in the window last night is Hannah. She's old now, and the only one left. She's lived by herself for fifty years. She hardly ever comes out of her house. I haven't ever even met her myself."

"But why? Why would someone want to be alone like that?" Amber asked.

"Fifty years ago, there was a terrible accident. Helen was killed," Mom said sadly. "They found her on a rock in the middle of that river we crossed over last night. She was only sixteen years old. Hannah was the one who found her. The sheriff said it was an accident. But soon everyone started rumors that Hannah had pushed Helen in. They had been angry at each other. They were both in love with the same boy.

Hannah heard people whispering about her at Helen's funeral. She ran away for a long time. Then she moved into that house next door, and hasn't spoken to anyone since."

Amber could not believe what she was hearing. A murder mystery! Right in her own family!

"But you don't need to worry about any of that," Mom said. "It happened a very long time ago. And old Miss McAfee keeps to herself. She's harmless. She'll never bother you. They say all she does is tend her garden. And play an old piano."

Amber and her mom got up, went over to the stove and fixed their plates.

It was very quiet out here in the country. Too quiet.

But all at once, Amber heard a very strange noise.

A loud roar came up their driveway. Amber could tell it was not a car. Suddenly it stopped with a loud screech.

Then a noise louder than anything Amber had ever heard shook the room.

BLAM!

Although she had never heard one, except on TV, Amber knew it was a gun.

32

Chapter Eleven

Amber and her mom dropped their plates and ran outside. Sheriff Johnson stood in the back yard holding a long shotgun. He leaned over and reached for something on the ground in front of him.

Amber gasped. He picked up a big, black snake.

"That fellow was heading straight for the house," he said, tossing the snake into the woods. "But you're lucky. It was just a chicken snake. Not anything that would hurt you. But I like to get rid of 'em anytime I see 'em."

Amber heard someone giggle. A chubby little girl stood next to Sheriff Johnson. She wore shorts, a T-shirt and a pair of flip flops. A pair of glasses sat on her nose. She looked like she might be just Amber's age.

"Hey!" she said, with an accent Amber had

never heard before. "My name's Kelly."

"This is my daughter," Sheriff Johnson said. "She heard you were here, Amber, and she wanted to come up and meet you."

Kelly had not ridden up to the house in a car. She'd ridden a strange-looking motorbike that now sat in the driveway. It wasn't a motorcycle, exactly. It had four wheels, not two. And it was kind of small.

Amber stared at the strange vehicle. What was really weird is that Kelly had obviously been driving it. And she sure didn't look old enough to drive!

Kelly noticed Amber's confusion.

"That's my four-wheeler," she said. "Don't you have one?"

Amber shook her head.

"Oh, wow! All the kids here have four-wheelers," Kelly said. "That's how we get around. Want to take a ride?"

Before Amber could say "No way," her mom jumped in.

"I think maybe Amber's had enough excitement," Mom said. "Why don't you girls come inside and get to know each other?"

Kelly looked up at her dad, who nodded that it was okay.

"I'll be heading back on into town now," he told Amber's mom. "But Kelly can stay here and play a while."

"Sure," Amber's mom said. "That would be great!"

Amber could tell Mom was trying hard to make her feel better. But she was not sure she wanted this Kelly girl forced on her. She didn't look like the friends Amber had had in New York. She didn't sound like them either.

She bet Kelly had never even been to Central Park. She probably didn't like to read, and never even painted her fingernails pink. Amber thought Kelly looked like a real tomboy.

But, Amber thought to herself, I'll give it a try.

Sheriff Johnson hopped in his patrol car. Just as he was about to drive away, he stopped.

"Oh, by the way," he said to Amber's mom. "I forgot to tell you. When I took Mark and David into town this morning to see about getting the car fixed, I got this strange message."

Chapter Twelve

Sheriff Johnson reached into his shirt pocket and pulled out a note.

"Somebody named Don called my office looking for you," he said. "He left a message that said, 'We're coming now.' What does that mean?"

"Oh, thank goodness!" Amber's mom sighed. "Don is the guy from the moving company. That means our furniture will get here today!"

Sheriff Johnson shook his head as if he didn't quite understand.

"Well, we don't have moving vans come into these parts much," he said. "I didn't know what the guy was talking about."

He pulled out of the driveway, leaving Amber and Kelly standing there staring at each other. Amber figured she needed to be nice.

"Uh, want to come in and see my room?" she

asked.

"Sure," Kelly said.

The girls headed into the house and climbed the old stairs to Amber's new room.

"Watch out," Amber said. "Don't step on that third step. There's a big hole there. David nearly killed himself last night when his foot went right through it."

Kelly climbed over the broken step, and held on tight to the old wooden railing. It wobbled back and forth in her hand.

"Looks like that step isn't the only thing that's going to need fixing," she mumbled.

The girls reached the top of the stairs, and Amber took Kelly down to her new room.

"Wow!" Kelly exclaimed, looking around the big, empty space. "This is downright spooky!"

Even though Amber felt the same way, it kind of made her mad to hear someone else say it.

"Well, it's going to look great in here once my bed's up and I put my posters on the wall. And see?" she said, walking over to the big window. "I'm going to hang my crystals right here. . . . Ouch!"

Pain shot up through Amber's leg like she had been cut by a knife. She sat down on the floor, about to cry. She grabbed her foot and looked at the bottom.

Kelly gasped.

"Blood! There's blood all over your foot!"

Chapter Thirteen

Amber looked down and saw blood pouring from just below her big toe. She was cut. Something sharp had ripped open her skin. It really hurt.

"Mrs. Elliston! Mrs. Elliston!" Kelly yelled down the stairs.

Soon Amber heard her mother's footsteps pounding up to her room.

"What is it? What's going on?" Mom gasped.

"Amber's cut her foot! And it's bleeding real bad," Kelly said.

"Let's take a look at that," Mom said, cupping Amber's foot in her hands. "Kelly. Go downstairs and bring me a wet paper towel."

Kelly rushed off. She returned in a minute holding a wet paper towel. Amber's mom wiped it gently over the cut, sopping up the blood.

"Oh, honey, this isn't so bad," she said.

"Looks like you just stubbed your foot on a splinter or something. These floors are so old. I bet that's what happened."

"I've got a first aid kit on my four-wheeler," Kelly said. "My dad makes us all carry one. That's the only way he'll let us drive 'em. I'll go get it."

As Kelly raced outside, Amber's mom hugged her hard. They rocked back and forth gently as Amber started to cry.

"I hate this place! I hate this place!" she whimpered. "I wish we had never come here! I want to go home!"

Kelly showed up with a red plastic box. She sat on the floor and popped open the top.

"See," she said. "Here's a band aid. And a bottle of Methiolade."

Amber's mom opened the bottle and swabbed the red stuff over the cut.

"Ouch!" Amber cried. "That stings!"

"Oh, it only lasts just a second," Kelly jumped in. "We have to use it all the time. You get lots of cuts and scrapes out here in the country. A lot of times I put it on spider bites or when a thorn gets me good in the leg."

Amber's mom could see that her daughter

wasn't happy. She peeled the plastic stickers off the band aid and placed it on the bottom of Amber's foot.

"See, that's helped already, hasn't it?" Mom asked.

Amber sniffled. But she had to admit her big accident was not that bad after all.

Suddenly there was a loud roar outside. People slammed car doors, and shouted to one another.

"Oh, my," Amber's mom gasped. "It's the movers! Sorry, honey. I've got to go downstairs and show them where to put everything. Will you be okay?"

Amber nodded. Mom raced out the door.

The two girls sat on the big seat underneath the tall window. Amber nursed her foot. Kelly started chatting.

"I'm going to be in the seventh grade next year. My dad says you will be, too," Kelly said. "We'll be in the same class, because there's only one class for each grade here. Won't that be fun? Maybe we can sit next to each other. I'll introduce you to everybody. And I'll teach you how to ride my four-wheeler. I bet they don't have those in New York City. That's where you're from, isn't it? My dad said you lived in New York."

Amber wasn't listening much. She kept staring at the spot on the floor where she had cut her foot.

How could that have happened, she wondered. No splinters poked up. The old wooden floor was worn completely smooth.

She looked more closely. She saw one board that seemed to be a bit higher than the others. Its edges stuck up about an inch above everything else.

"That's what did it!" she cried. "I dragged my foot across that old floorboard."

Kelly stopped talking.

"Why is it sticking out like that?" she asked.

The girls got very quiet. Amber got up and walked over to the funny spot in the floor. She pushed her other foot against the strange board.

Whoosh!

It popped open.

Chapter Fourteen

Two girls peered down into a small, secret hole hidden underneath the floor.

They stared into the secret compartment. A piece of paper lay there, tied up in a faded pink ribbon. It looked very old.

"What is that?" Kelly asked.

"Shush," Amber said. "Be quiet."

She screwed up her courage, reached her hand into the dark hole, and pulled the paper out.

"A letter!" Kelly gasped. "It's an old letter!"

Amber held the crumbling note in her hand. She turned it over several times, examining the treasure she had just found.

"Should we open it?" Kelly asked. "I wonder what it says? Or who wrote it? Or how long it has been here?"

"Well, Mom said no one has lived in this house

in fifty years," Amber said. "So it must be really old."

Amber walked back to the window seat and held the old note up to the light. It was written on paper that had once been pale blue. It had nearly faded to white.

Eerie, ancient-looking handwriting adorned the front. It didn't look like the loopy cursive Amber had learned in the third grade. The words looked more like something off an old map. Or like those signatures she had seen at the bottom of the Constitution the summer her family had visited Washington, D.C.

"Look at that stamp," Kelly whispered. "I've never seen any like that before!"

Amber didn't recognize the picture on the old stamp. She did notice it only cost two cents. She looked closely at the handwriting on the front. The letter was addressed to Helen McAfee.

"It's from 1945," she told Kelly. "That would have been around the time of the accident."

Amber decided to hold the letter up to the light that streamed in through the big window. She saw a black spot right in the middle.

The spot started to move.

All of sudden, the black spot jumped out of the old letter and landed on Amber's face!

Chapter Fifteen

"Eeeeek!" Amber screamed, brushing her face wildly with her hands.

Kelly jumped up and stamped her foot hard on the floor.

"A Palmetto bug," she said. "It was a Palmetto bug."

Amber stared at her new friend.

"They're all over the place here," Kelly explained. "They're really big, and they look really scary. But they won't hurt you. The grossest thing about them is the way they look after they've been squashed."

Amber looked down at the greasy, yellow guts on the floor.

"Yuck!" she said. "That's worse than the roaches we had back in New York."

She picked up one of the paper towels her

mom had used to nurse her foot and wiped the bug guts off the floor.

"Amber, there's something I want to ask you," Kelly said.

"Sure," Amber said, tossing the dead bug in the corner.

"So, you know about the accident, huh?" Kelly asked.

"Not much," Amber said. "Just what my mom told me last night."

"Well," Kelly continued. "I wasn't going to say anything to you. But everyone has always said this house is haunted. They say the ghost of Helen McAfee walks here at night. Some kids say they have seen her out on the hill, wearing a white dress. Sometimes she picks flowers. She puts them in her hair. But she disappears before anyone can get close. She was killed, you know. Down by that big tree your family almost hit last night by the river. Her crazy sister, Old Miss McAfee, lives right there. Right next door to you."

Amber got very quiet.

"What? What is it?" Kelly asked.

"We saw a girl down by that tree last night," Amber said. "That's why we had the accident. My dad was trying to keep from hitting her. She was standing all alone in the rain. And you know what's weird? She had on a white party dress. And a flower in her hair."

Kelly stared at Amber. Suddenly, she grabbed the letter and pulled on the pink ribbon. The note unfolded, and the girls stared at the first lines written on the paper.

"Come to me, come to me, oh beautiful one. Come to me, or I shall come to you."

Before the girls could read the rest of the letter, a gust of wind blew through the window. It swept the letter out of their hands and sent it fluttering to the floor.

Amber jumped down to retrieve her treasure. Another blast of wind blew the letter back into the secret hole in the floor. Without thinking, Amber stuck her hand down inside to pull it out.

Then she froze. Something touched her fingers.

Something alive!

Chapter Sixteen

Amber screamed. She yanked her hand back from the black hole.

"What was that?" she shrieked.

Kelly rushed over and peeked in.

"Oooooh!" she yelled. "It's a rat!"

This was too much for Amber. Rats were supposed to live in New York City, not out here in the country. Her dad had promised it would be safe here. He said they were coming to Jackson because of all the crime and trouble in the big city.

Well, Amber had never touched a rat in New York City. And certainly not in her own house!

"Hey, don't get so upset," Kelly said. "I was just teasing you. It's not a rat. It's just a mouse. You find them out in the country all the time. We've got 'em in our house, too. My dad just sets traps, and that takes care of them. It won't hurt you."

Amber did not think Kelly's joke was funny at all. But before she could get too mad, she heard her mother calling from downstairs.

"Girls! Girls!" her mom hollered. "Come down here. I need you to run an errand for me."

Amber stared straight into Kelly's freckled, round face.

"Don't tell anyone about this," Amber said holding up the letter.

"Okay," Kelly said. "I won't."

Amber certainly didn't want to put her hand back into that hole. So she grabbed the faded blue letter and stuffed it into her pocket.

I'll finish reading it later, she thought.

The girls ran down the stairs into the kitchen. Amber's mom was busy telling the movers where to put all the boxes. They had already brought in the kitchen table, and some chairs.

"Yeah!" Amber shouted. "It's our stuff! Our table! Our chairs! They're finally here!"

Amber's mom motioned for her to quiet down.

"Listen," she said. "It's just crazy around here. It's going to take hours for the movers to unload everything, so why don't you girls do me a favor?"

Amber and Kelly listened.

"I want you to walk down to the mailbox. It's right at the foot of the hill," Mom said. "You know — right next to Old Miss McAfee's house."

Chapter Seventeen

Amber's mom reached into her purse and pulled out several letters.

Actually, Amber realized, they were bills. One was to the gas company. Another to the phone company. And one to the electricity people.

"I've got to get these in the mail today or we'll be in trouble," Amber's mom laughed. "We don't want them to shut off the lights before we even get moved in! Take these down to the mailbox, and put them in. Amber, you don't know this, but you've got to raise up the red flag to let the mailman know there's something waiting for him."

They didn't have to do things like that to mail bills in New York. At Amber's old home, they'd had a post office box down in the lobby of her building. Not one of these big black mailboxes that sat by the side of the road.

"Oh, don't worry Mrs. Elliston," Kelly piped up. "I know all about how to get your bills on their way."

Amber's mom handed the bills to her daughter just as the movers headed through the door with the living room sofa.

"Run along now," Mom said. "I'll see you later."

Amber stuffed the bills into her pocket and headed out the door with Kelly. They started walking down the long hill when, suddenly, Kelly stopped.

"This is stupid," she said. "Let's ride my four-wheeler!"

"I don't think we should," Amber said, knowing her mom would not approve one bit.

"Oh, it's okay," Kelly urged. "I ride it all the time. There's room for you on the back. That way we can get there in half the time."

Amber got a sick feeling in the pit of her stomach. She knew her mother would not want her on that strange bike. Then again, Amber didn't feel like taking a long hike into a place she had never been before. It *would* be a lot faster.

And maybe, Amber thought secretly, it might be kind of fun.

The girls headed back up the driveway. Kelly climbed on the four-wheeler, and motioned Amber to hop on behind her. With the flip of a switch, the machine fired up.

"Hold on!" Kelly said with a laugh.

Then something happened that made Amber feel more afraid than she had ever felt in her life.

Chapter Eighteen

She felt like she was going to die.

Forget the car accident the night before. Or the time she had fallen down the stairs in her old apartment building. Or even when they'd had to give her that big shot in her mouth to pull her teeth.

Amber felt as if her body was totally out of control, going so fast that she was sure to be killed.

Here she was, with a girl she hardly even knew, hurtling down the hill at breakneck speed. Amber was terrified. They went faster than she had expected, dizzyingly fast — faster than she had ever gone on the bike path in the park. Trees whizzed by. She held onto Kelly tightly as they zipped around corners and bounced over bumps in the gravel road.

It seemed like forever, but soon Kelly slowed the four-wheeler to a stop. The girls were sitting in front of two mailboxes.

"Here it is," Kelly said with a grin. "Stick your stuff inside. Then let's *really* do some riding."

Amber was relieved. She hadn't died. She hadn't even fallen off!

With a sigh of relief, she reached into her pocket, pulled out the bills, and placed them in the mailbox. She even remembered to put up the red flag her mom had told her about.

Without warning, Kelly started up the four-wheeler. In seconds, the girls were zipping down a rough trail off the main road. It wound through the woods, by a creek, and past an old barn. Amber could see someone's garden up ahead. It was filled with rows of corn, marigolds and other green things.

"Oh my gosh!" Amber yelled suddenly. "Kelly! Kelly! Stop this thing!"

Kelly slowed to a stop.

"You know what I did?" Amber said in a panic. "I put that old letter in the mailbox with Mom's bills! We've got to go back and get it!"

Without a word, Kelly turned the four-wheeler around and headed back to the road. Just as they approached the mailbox, she pulled behind a bush and turned off the engine.

"Oh no!" she said. "There's the mailman!"

A man with a baseball hat was driving a big, old green car down the shoulder of the road. He was sitting on the passenger's side, with his hand stretched way over to the steering wheel.

How could he drive a car like that, Amber wondered.

He leaned over to the mailbox and pulled out the stack of bills — and the old letter. He put them all in his big mail pouch. Amber and Kelly sat silently as he drove away.

"Well, I guess we'll never get to know what was in that letter," Kelly said with a sigh. "Maybe it was from Old Miss McAfee. Maybe she was threatening to murder her sister! Maybe she had written that she was going to kill her, and *we* would have solved the crime!"

Just as Amber was going to tell Kelly to shut up, she froze.

Someone put a hand on her shoulder. Someone with bony fingers and long chipped fingernails.

Someone whose hand looked like that of a witch!

Chapter Nineteen

Amber looked up at the person who held her shoulder so tightly.

It was an old woman. Amber had seen her somewhere before. Now she remembered — it was that white hair that hung down below the woman's waist. And those coal black eyes.

It was the woman she had seen in the window the night before!

Just as Amber was about to shriek, Kelly gunned the four-wheeler.

The girls zoomed out from behind the bushes. Kelly wheeled the bike as fast as it could go down the dirt path. Soon, they were back out on the main road. They zipped past the mailboxes, back up the road toward Amber's house.

Suddenly, Kelly pulled over and stopped.

"Oh my gosh," she said. "That was old Miss

McAfee!"

"Wow. I thought it was a witch," Amber sighed. "I thought we were done for."

"No, she's never hurt anybody. She's just kind of strange and creepy," Kelly said. "Funny, though. She *never* comes out to talk to anyone. Much less touch them. She must have been really mad at us."

Kelly and Amber sat on the bike at the side of the road for what seemed like a very long time. They didn't say anything to each other.

But that was okay. Although they had just met, somehow they knew they were going to be great friends. Being great friends means that sometimes you don't have to talk at all.

The sun was high above the fields. Amber heard the chirping of birds all around her. That was something she hadn't heard a lot in New York City.

Kelly leaned back and let the sun shine on her face. Amber did the same thing, trying to rest from her scare.

"I think I'd better go home now," Amber said.

Just as Kelly reached down to fire up the four-wheeler, the girls heard something strange.

It was piano music.

It began very softly. Then it got louder and

louder, as if someone was pounding on the keys. The music was old and sad.

"Gosh, that's creepy," Kelly said, starting to go.

"No. Wait!" Amber gasped. "I've heard that somewhere before."

A high, wailing voice began to sing.

"Come to me, come to me, oh beautiful one. Come to me, or I shall come to you."

Chapter Twenty

Kelly pulled the four-wheeler back onto the main road as fast as she could.

The girls sped up the hill. They were so frightened they didn't even try to hide that Amber had been on the bike without her mom's permission.

Amber's mom was standing on the front porch with her arms folded.

"Amber Elliston!" she said. She always called Amber by both names when she was mad. "Who told you you could ride on that bike with Kelly? Those things are really dangerous if you don't know what you're doing. And you weren't even wearing a helmet!"

Amber looked down and said nothing.

"It's my fault, Mrs. Elliston," Kelly said. "I talked Amber into riding with me. It's really not as bad as you think. All the kids out here ride four-wheelers."

Wow, Amber thought. Kelly is a good friend to stick up for me like that.

"Well, I don't care what all the other kids do," Mom said. "Do not *ever* get on that thing again until your dad or Sheriff Johnson can give you a safety lesson. Kelly, I think it's time for you to go home now."

Amber climbed off the bike and waved at Kelly as she drove down the drive. Just as Kelly reached the main road to town, Amber saw a familiar car turn into the driveway.

It was Dad and David. And the Honda!

They pulled up to the house and parked behind the moving van. David hopped out excitedly.

"Look! We got our car fixed!" he said.

"We were really lucky," Dad said, shutting the car door. "No major damage. They just had to replace the windshield."

"And guess what?" David added. "I've been bitten by a shark!"

Chapter Twenty-One

As Amber stared at her brother, he started laughing.

"Oh, David, quit teasing your sister," Dad said. "What David is trying to tell you is that he's *become* a shark. A Jackson Shark. David's now a member of the Jackson Swim Team!"

As the family went into the house, David told them how he had walked around town while the car was being repaired.

"There's a big pool right near Dad's new office," he said. "They were signing people up for the summer swim team. We start practice tomorrow."

David had been swimming since he was a baby. He had been on the swim team at his old school in New York. In fact, one of the things he had hated most about moving was leaving his swim team.

Even though he drove her crazy most of the

time, Amber couldn't help being happy that David was going to make some new friends, too.

Amber looked around the house. It was starting to feel like home. All their living room furniture was arranged neatly around the old fireplace.

Amber raced up the stairs to her room. There it was! Her bed! Her stuffed animals! Her books and posters!

She lay down on her bedspread with the pink flowers, curled up and fell asleep.

Hours later, when she woke, it was night. She went downstairs, and made herself a peanut butter and jelly sandwich. David was already asleep in his room. So was her dad.

Amber found her mom in a small room at the back of the house, hunched over her computer.

"Hi honey," Mom said. "Guess you can tell this is going to be my office."

She was drawing the illustrations for a new children's book.

"Were you able to get some sleep?" Mom asked, stifling a yawn.

"Yeah, I guess so," Amber said. "But I feel wide awake now."

"Tell you what," Mom said. "I think I'm going

to head to bed myself. But if you want to, why don't you play around on the computer for a while? It's okay. And guess what? We've even got our E-mail up and running — way out here in the country!"

Amber sat down. Her mom bent over and kissed her goodnight.

Amber stared at the menu on the screen. She clicked on the E-mail program and heard the familiar sound of the modem hooking into the phone line. She entered her password, and watched the color picture of a mail box flash on.

She was surprised when the flat computer voice said, "You've Got Mail."

Who would this be from, Amber thought. None of my friends in New York know my E-mail address.

For some reason, her girlfriends had just never gotten into computers. Usually, Amber just sent computer messages to fan clubs of her favorite music artists. None of them ever messaged back.

Amber clicked on the mailbox, and a message appeared.

Suddenly, Amber could not move. She felt frozen in place. A shiver ran down her spine as she read the words:

"Come to me, come to me, oh beautiful one. Come to me, or I shall come to you."

A photograph started to materialize on the screen. It was very old. First Amber saw blonde, curly hair. Then the face of a young girl emerged, with bright, painted lips.

She had a flower in her hair!

Just as Amber was about to run from the room, the picture moved. The girl in the photo turned her head slowly, looked straight into Amber's eyes and said:

"Help me. Help me. Help me help her."

Chapter Twenty-Two

Amber switched off the computer and ran straight to her bedroom.

She snuggled between her pink sheets. Soon, she was sleeping like a baby. She didn't stir until she heard the *clunk-clunk-clunk* of David's big tennis shoes on the stairs the next morning.

"Amber! Amber!" David shouted. "Get up and get down here for breakfast!"

Still in her nightgown, Amber trotted down the stairs to the kitchen.

Mom had a big breakfast spread all over the table. It was Amber's favorite — French toast, with lots of syrup and butter. She sat down at the table with her mom, dad and David. It had been a long time since the family had been able to do this.

"What time did you finally get to sleep last night?" Mom asked.

"Oh, I went to bed right after you did," Amber said.

"Didn't you get the computer to work?" Mom asked. "It was doing fine when I was on it."

"Yeah, it worked okay," Amber said nervously. "Uh, I just didn't feel like messing with it very long."

Amber sat quietly, thinking.

Should she tell her mom what she had seen on the screen?

No, she decided. She would just say I was dreaming, like she did when I saw that face in the car.

The family finished breakfast, and cleaned up together. It was great to have all their things on the shelves and in the cabinets. Even David seemed happy and talkative.

"Hey, Sis!" he said.

He must be in a really good mood, Amber thought. He hadn't called her "Sis" in years.

"Want to go exploring?" he asked.

Amber wasn't sure why David was being chummy all of a sudden. He usually didn't want to have anything to do with her. But she said, "Sure."

She ran upstairs, changed into her shorts, and found David out on the front porch. They started walking down the hill.

"Hey, kids!" Mom yelled as they were about to turn onto the main road. "Would you check the mail for me? I'm hoping my magazines will show up today."

They walked to the mailbox by Old Miss McAfee's house.

Amber peeked inside, but saw nothing that looked like a magazine. She stuck her hand deep into the back, just to be sure.

She felt a small piece of paper and pulled it out. It was a letter, on pale blue stationery. It looked very old. There was no return address.

Then Amber felt a lump in her throat. She stared at the front of the letter. The handwriting was the same as she had seen on the note in her room the day before. So was the stamp!

And the letter was addressed to Amber Elliston.

Chapter Twenty-Three

David stared at his sister. He knew something was very wrong.

"What is it?" he asked. "What's that old letter? And why is it addressed to you?"

Amber tore open the envelope and read the short message inside. It said: *"Go with your brother today. Help me. Help me. Help her."*

David and Amber stood in front of the mailbox in silence. They stared at the letter for a long time.

Finally. David put his hand on Amber's shoulder.

"Listen, Sis," he said. "There's something I've got to tell you. Some really weird things have been happening to me ever since we got here. I've heard that message before."

Amber looked up at her brother, wanting to hear more.

"Remember that night in the car when you saw that face in the window?" he said.

"Yes," Amber nodded.

"Well, I saw it, too," he said. "And the girl by the tree just before we had the accident? I saw her, too. Then last night, after I went to bed, I heard someone crying. I got up to see what it was, and looked out my window. I saw that same girl walking on the hill down from our house. She looked up at me and said: *"Help me. Help me. Help her."*

David paused.

"Amber, I don't want to scare you," he said. "But I think it's a ghost."

Amber felt more relieved than scared. She had someone who would believe her, who would not think she was nuts.

She poured out her whole story to David. She told him about the computer message, and the photograph that had talked to her. She told him about the letter she had found in the floor of her room. And the strange song she kept hearing.

"And David, what's even creepier is the story behind all this," she said.

Just as she was about to tell him the tale of Helen McAfee and how she died, he interrupted.

"I know all about it," he said. "When I was down at the swimming pool yesterday, I met some guys who are going to be in my class next year. I told them where I was living, and they got really funny looks on their faces. They said our house is haunted! They told me how Helen McAfee was found dead on a rock in the river a long time ago. And how everyone blamed her sister Hannah. And that's why Old Miss McAfee lives here alone. And has for fifty years."

"I saw her!" Amber cried. "I saw her yesterday! She grabbed me when Kelly and I were down here on the four-wheeler. It nearly scared me to death! She looks just like a witch!"

David kicked his shoe into the dirt, and thought a minute.

"Listen, the reason I wanted to go exploring today was I know where it all happened," he said. "Remember that tree by the river where we had the wreck? Well, the guys in town told me that, years ago, that used to be the old swimming hole. There used to be an old rope swing tied to that tree. Everyone would swing on it and jump into the river. That's where Helen McAfee fell — or was pushed. No one has gone swimming there since. I want to go down there and check it out."

"Well, someone is trying to tell us something," Amber said. "Maybe it's a ghost — the ghost of Helen McAfee. And maybe we'd better start listening to her."

Chapter Twenty-Four

Amber and David started walking down the gravel road toward the river.

It was a long hike — maybe two miles. They said nothing to each other along the way. The sun overhead got hotter and hotter.

Gosh, Amber thought. I thought New York was hot in the summer. That's nothing compared to this.

David swatted a mosquito. Beads of sweat dripped down his face.

They passed a few farmhouses, and several old barns that had fallen down. Cows grazed in the fields. A skunk ran across the road.

After half an hour, they rounded a corner. The road sloped down into open country, with huge fields of corn. In the distance, they saw the one-lane bridge over the river. The metal across the top of it zigzagged like something made out of Legos.

"Look!" David said. "That's it! That's the tree!"

Next to the bridge, an enormous oak stood tall against the sky. It hung over the river like a big green claw. The trunk was huge.

"Oh my gosh!" Amber gasped. "What if we had hit that thing when we swerved?"

"We'd all be dead," David said softly. Suddenly, he started running.

"Wait! Wait for me!" Amber cried, racing along behind him.

It only took a minute to reach the bridge. David and Amber walked slowly onto the old wooden planks, and looked at the water swirling furiously beneath them.

"I can't believe kids used to swim in there," Amber said. "Wouldn't it be really dangerous?"

"I guess that's why they don't do it anymore," David answered. "And why Helen McAfee got killed."

Just as they were about to head over to look at the tree, they heard the sound of a four-wheeler. It was Kelly.

"Hey! What are y'all doing?" she called as she drove over the bridge.

"Come here," Amber said. "I want to show you something."

She pulled the ghost letter out of her pocket and handed it to Kelly.

"Wow!" Kelly gasped. "Where did you get this?"

"It came in the mail," Amber said. "Today."

Kelly looked up at David, as if she were not sure it was OK to talk in front of him.

"It's okay," Amber said. "He knows all about it. And guess what? He's seen the ghost, too!"

"We came down here to look at the spot where Helen McAfee died," David said.

Kelly pointed to a big rock sitting in the middle of the water. The river bubbled around it furiously on either side.

"It was right down there," Kelly said. "Let's get a closer look."

Before David and Amber could say no, Kelly parked her four-wheeler and headed across the river bank to the old tree. Without thinking, David and Amber followed.

The three of them crawled over the huge roots, which curled up like fat snakes sticking out of the ground. They walked around to the side of the tree facing the river, and looked down.

There it was. The spot where Helen McAfee died!

Chapter Twenty-Five

The big, flat rock stuck up through the green water like a small island. The water around it was very fast and deep.

There was a steep drop from the tree down to the river below. There was no sign of life anywhere.

Suddenly, David whispered "Get down!"

The three of them crouched behind the bushes around the tree roots.

"What?" Kelly asked. "What is it?"

"Look. Over there," David said. He pointed to the woods on the other side.

At first Amber saw nothing. But as her eyes focused, she saw a thin stream of smoke rising above the trees.

"Maybe it's some guys fishing," Kelly said. "Maybe they've made a campfire or something."

A man stepped out of the woods. And he

wasn't carrying a fishing pole.

He was very big, with long gray hair that looked as if it had not been combed in years. He had a scraggly beard. His clothes were dirty.

Right behind him was the meanest looking dog Amber had ever seen. It barked and growled, and chewed on an old tin can.

"A pit bull," Kelly whispered. "That's a pit bulldog!"

As the three of them watched in silence, their hearts pounding, the man reached into his shirt pocket and pulled out a pale blue piece of paper.

It was a letter. He stared at it for a moment, then ripped it into tiny pieces.

He threw them into the water, and let out a bloodcurdling scream.

Chapter Twenty-Six

Without a word, the kids jumped from their hiding place and ran back to the road as fast as they could.

David and Amber kept going, racing toward their house. Kelly hopped on the four-wheeler, and soon caught up with them.

"Who was that?" Amber asked, out of breath.

"I have no idea," Kelly said. "And I've lived here all my life. I've never seen that guy before. I didn't think anyone lived down here by the river."

"Listen," David said, very seriously. "I think that guy is dangerous. And I think he might have seen us."

The three kids stared at each other, wondering what to do.

Then David said he had a plan.

"Amber, we need to get home as fast as possible," he said. "But we've also got to get to the bottom of this. I've got an idea. My dad works at the newspaper. Maybe we could go down to his office and look up the newspapers from fifty years ago. Those old stories might help us find out what really happened to Helen McAfee. And maybe someone there can tell us who that man is. And how he's connected to all this."

Amber and Kelly nodded.

"I've got to eat lunch with my grandma today," Kelly said. "But I could meet you later this afternoon. Maybe around three?"

"That would work," David answered. "I've got swim team practice, but it gets out about that time. Amber, that leaves you. You've got to figure out a way to get Mom to drive you into town. Then you can meet us at Dad's office."

"Mom promised she'd take me to the Wal-Mart to buy some new curtains for my room," Amber said. "I'll get her to drop me off at the paper."

All three of them looked at the river one last time. They didn't see anything. All they heard was water rushing under the bridge. A hawk flew overhead.

Kelly turned her four-wheeler around and headed towards town. Amber and David started their long walk home. They stared at the ground, not saying a word.

They heard a dog bark.

It was not a friendly bark, like the yip-yip of the little poodle that used to live down the hall from them in New York. This bark sounded mean and wild.

Amber and David turned and looked back.

There it was, under the tree. It was the pit bull they had seen on the other side of the river. He barked furiously, as if he wanted to run at them but something was holding him back. He lurched and jumped uncontrollably.

"Do you see what I see?" David asked.

Amber squinted. Her eyes followed the taught rope that was around the dog's neck. It led back behind the old oak tree.

Suddenly, someone stepped out from behind the trunk.

It was the crazy man. He jerked the dog's collar back with a force so strong it made the dog whimper.

Then he looked straight at Amber and David.

Chapter Twenty-Seven

"Let's get out of here!" David cried.

Amber and David ran the nearly two miles home. They were sweating and panting by the time they reached the old mailboxes.

David stopped and squatted on the ground, out of breath.

"David, I'm really scared!" Amber whimpered. "I think maybe we're in big trouble."

"As crazy as he looks, that guy didn't follow us," David said. "He didn't turn his dog loose on us or anything. So I don't think he's going to hurt us. He doesn't even know who we are."

"Yeah, but did you see what he threw into the river?" Amber asked. "It was a letter! A letter that looked just like this one!"

Amber reached into her pocket and pulled out the mysterious note. She unfolded it and read it again.

"*Go with your brother today. Help me. Help me. Help her,*" she read. "What do you suppose that means?"

"Obviously, someone wanted us to see that guy," David answered. "But help her? Who is her?"

Just then, they heard something very creepy.

Piano music.

The same piano music Amber had heard when she was at Old Miss McAfee's place with Kelly.

David looked up and saw Amber staring at him.

"I know," he said. "It's that song that was on the car radio the night we got here. I've been hearing her play it every night. Let's get home, and get into town as fast as we can."

They walked up the hill to their house. They were too tired to run any more. Their mom was on the front porch, planting red flowers in big ceramic pots. She looked up at them and smiled.

"Did you get to see some of this beautiful country?" she asked.

Amber and David just nodded.

"You got back just in time," Mom said. "David, I've got to drive you into town for your swimming lesson. Run upstairs and get your swim trunks. There are some towels in the bathroom. And don't forget the sunscreen!"

Amber knew this was her chance.

"Mom? Can I go with you?" she asked. "You said you'd take me to Wal-Mart to get some curtains for that big window in my room. Could we maybe do that today?"

Amber's mom seemed irritated. Then she looked at her hot and tired daughter, and changed her mind.

"Sure, honey. Sure," she said. "I've got to pick up some computer supplies anyway. I'll drop you off at the store and you can look around."

The Ellistons piled into the black Honda. Except for a few scratches on the hood, it seemed as good as new, in spite of the accident. They drove away from their house, back onto a paved road and into the small town of Jackson.

Amber had seen small towns before, but mainly on TV. This one was actually smaller than she had even imagined. A few stores formed a square around an old courthouse. Most of the stores were empty and closed.

Amber's mom drove a few blocks farther, and pulled the car into a huge parking lot. There stood a giant Wal-Mart. Next to it was the community swimming pool.

David hopped out of the car.

"See you later," he yelled as he walked toward the pool. "Wish me luck!"

"Amber, you go on into the store. Ask someone where you can find the curtains, and see if there is anything you like," Mom said. "I've got to drive over to the next town for my things. There's no computer store in Jackson. It will probably take me a couple of hours, but you can browse. Or if you get tired of that, why don't you walk down to Daddy's new office? It's just across from the courthouse. You'll recognize it. It's an old building that says 'Jackson County News' on the front door."

Wow, Amber thought. This couldn't have worked out more perfectly.

Chapter Twenty-Eight

Amber walked through the sprawling Wal-Mart for a few minutes.

She didn't even go to where the curtains were displayed. Instead, she walked up and down the aisles where the toys were. She thought about buying a new board game. Or an outfit for her Barbie. But, somehow, she couldn't keep her mind on toys.

I've got to get down to the newspaper office, she thought.

She looked at her watch. An hour had gone by. She headed out the door of the store.

Just as she started walking down the street, she heard a familiar voice.

"Hey!" It was Kelly.

Amber hardly recognized her here in town. It occurred to her that this was the first time she had seen Kelly without her four-wheeler.

"Where's your bike?" Amber asked.

"I just use that for riding out in the country," Kelly said. "My dad won't let me ride it in town. Too many cars. You on your way to the newspaper?"

"Yeah," Amber said. "David should be getting out of swim practice any minute. I'm dying to get a look at the old stories about Helen McAfee, and how she died."

The girls headed off together.

The newspaper office occupied a very old building. Amber thought it looked run down. It didn't seem anything like the big office of the New York Times, where her dad used to work. It made Amber kind of sad.

Kelly pushed the door and walked in.

A middle-aged woman with big blond hair sat behind the counter. She had very long red fingernails. She was smoking a cigarette.

Yuck! Amber thought. Most of the offices in New York didn't allow people to smoke at work.

"Hey Kelly. How are you doing?" the woman said, smiling.

"Just fine," Kelly said. "Joanne, this is Amber. Her dad is the new editor here."

"Well, sugar, how nice to meet you!" Joanne

said, standing up. She leaned over the counter and gave Amber a big hug.

"We just love your daddy," she went on. "He's going to do great things for this town. He's right back there in his office if you want to go see him."

Amber and Kelly didn't say anything. Amber didn't know what to say. How was she supposed to tell this Joanne woman with the big hair what they really wanted? Just as she was about to screw up the courage to ask to see the stories on Helen McAfee, David burst in the door.

"Hi!" he said confidently.

Even though he didn't talk very much, David always seemed to know how to get along with people.

"I'm David Elliston."

"Then you're Amber's brother!" Joanne gushed. "Glad to meet you. Guess you kids want to see Mr. Elliston. Let me go get him for you."

"Actually, there's something else we'd like to see," David said.

"Oh, really? What's that?" Joanne asked.

"Do you keep copies of old newspapers here? Ones from a really long time ago?" he asked.

"Yes. They're all in the back. We keep them in big books. And they go back a long time. This news-big books. And they go back a long time. This newspaper has been around since 1922," Joanne bragged. "Whatcha looking for?"

"Do you have the ones from 1945?" David asked.

"You bet!" Joanne said. "Let's go see what we can find."

Joanne led the kids behind the counter, down a narrow hall, and past their dad's office. They could see him working at a big desk. He was talking to someone on the phone, and didn't notice them. They ended up in a tiny storage room lined from floor to ceiling with huge leather books filled with yellowing newspapers.

Joanne ran her fingers down the spines. The side of each book was stamped in gold with a date.

"Let's see," she said, going down the stack. "1949, 1948, 1947, 1946. Oh! Here it is. 1945!"

David helped Joanne pull the big book from its place on the shelf. They plopped it on a big table in the center of the room. It smelled very old. David opened it up and started thumbing carefully through the pages.

These old newspapers did not look anything like the ones published today. They were mostly words — very few pictures, and no colors.

The news back then was all about World War

II. Amber remembered that her grandfather had fought in World War II. Like her grandmother, he had died before she was even born.

David turned the pages through the months. April. May. June. July. Nothing. Absolutely nothing about Helen McAfee.

Just as the kids were reaching the end of the book, David flipped the page over to August 26, 1945.

Amber gasped.

On the front page of the paper, the headline said "Local Girl Killed in River Accident."

Underneath it was something Amber could not believe.

A photograph showed a young girl with curly blond hair. There was a flower in her hair. The caption said "Helen McAfee."

It was the same photograph Amber had seen on her computer screen.

Chapter Twenty-Nine

Amber, David and Kelly stared at the old photo.

"Wow," Kelly said. "She was really pretty!"

David started reading aloud.

"Helen McAfee, 16, was found dead in the Jackson River yesterday morning. She was lying on a rock near the Jackson County Bridge. The cause of death was apparently a head injury. Authorities said the young woman did not drown.

"McAfee, a sophomore at Jackson County High, had been missing for nearly 24 hours. She was discovered by a group of boys. Her sister, Hannah McAfee, who had also been missing, came forward shortly after workers removed the body from the river. She said she didn't know anything about her sister's accident, or what had happened.

"The sheriff's office has ruled this an acci-

dental death. Services will be held at the Smith-Austin funeral home on Saturday."

"Well, that doesn't tell us much," David said.

"But what about that part about Hannah being missing too?" Amber wondered out loud. "That's kind of strange. Why would she have disappeared?"

A sharp, raspy voice cut in.

"Cause she did it."

Chapter Thirty

It was Joanne, the receptionist.

She had overheard the conversation. She looked at the old paper with the kids.

"No one ever got to the bottom of it," Joanne said. "But pretty soon after this happened, pieces of the story started coming out. Everybody around here thinks Hannah pushed Helen into the river. She was mad at her. They were both in love with an orphan boy named Jim who had come here for the summer to stay with some relatives. Both of those McAfee girls just went crazy for him. They say he was very good looking."

"But why would people think Hannah would actually kill her own sister?" Amber asked.

"Jealousy," Joanne said, flicking another cigarette. "See, this Jim played the guitar. And Helen wanted to be a singer. They hit it off right away. They

93

would sit down by the river singing songs and holding hands. Hannah was furious. She liked music, too. I think she played the piano. They say she even wrote a song for Jim. And that's when it really got bad."

"What do you mean?" asked Kelly.

"The night Helen McAfee disappeared, there was a talent show down at the high school. My mother was there, and she told me all about it. Hannah McAfee was going to play the piano. Helen was the singer. She was really pretty, you know. Always wore a white flower in her hair.

"Well, right before they started, Hannah got up and said she was dedicating the song to a boy named Jim," Joanne continued. "Helen was furious. She was so mad she couldn't even sing the song. She ran from the stage. Hannah followed her. They had a huge fight out in front of the school. People say Hannah screamed at Helen that she hated her so much she could kill her! That was the last time anyone ever saw Helen alive."

"What was the song?" David asked.

"Oh, gosh," Joanne said. "I don't remember."

Then she thought a moment.

"Here, let's look," she said, flipping back to the paper from the week before. She thumbed through the old pages, then stopped at the bottom of page six.

"See, here's a story about the upcoming talent show."

She ran her fingers down the names of the students who would be performing. There she was — Helen McAfee. The story also listed the song she would be singing.

It was "Come to Me My Beautiful One."

The lights in the tiny room suddenly went out. It was so dark Amber couldn't even see her hand in front of her face.

It seemed as black as death.

Chapter Thirty-One

No one moved.

Suddenly, Amber saw the glow of Joanne's cigarette.

"Darn!" the receptionist blurted. "Those stupid lights! They go out every time Ed runs the presses."

Amber, David and Kelly watched the glow of Joanne's cigarette travel to the far corner of the room. She opened the door. The rest of the office was dark too, except for a beam of light heading down the hall towards them.

"Joanne? Joanne?"

It was their dad's voice. He was carrying a flashlight. The beam hit Amber and David right in the face.

"Kids! What are you doing here?" he asked.

"We were just in that back room looking at some old newspapers," David said.

"Yeah, and then the lights went out!" Amber

piped up.

"Well, I guess this is kind of a bad time for your visit," Amber's dad said. "Seems like every time they start running the presses in the back, it cuts the power. Too bad. I'd really like to show you my new office."

They heard a click down the hall. Joanne had flipped a big switch in an old box in the wall. At once, light filled the office again.

"I was just about to close up for the day," Dad said. "Where's your mom? Do you kids need a ride home?"

Right then, Carol Elliston walked through the front door.

"So, what do you think of your dad's new place?" she asked, a big smile on her face.

The kids stood silently. Amber was still disappointed that the office was so much smaller than the one at The New York Times.

"Mom, is it okay if Kelly spends the night?" Amber asked, changing the subject.

"As long as it's all right with her parents," Mom replied.

"I'll call and ask," Kelly said. "I'm sure my dad won't mind."

Kelly phoned her house, and got the go ahead to spend the night with Amber. She headed out the door with the Ellistons, and they all piled into the Honda.

"I'll lock up Mr. Elliston," Joanne called out the door. Then she added, "Did you kids find what you were looking for?"

Amber and David nodded.

As they drove through town, they passed the Wal-Mart, the swimming pool and Jackson County High School.

"Look," Mom said. "That's where David will go to school this fall."

It was a very old building, surrounded by huge trees and covered in ivy. A sign out front had black, plastic letters that could be moved around to spell different things. The message today said, "Back to School August 30."

Darn, Amber thought. That's so soon. Summer's almost over.

As the Honda passed the school, Amber turned around and looked at the other side of the sign. There was a different message on that side of the sign.

It said, "Talent Show Tonight. Starring Helen McAfee."

Chapter Thirty-Two

"David, Kelly, look!" Amber whispered.

The kids turned around in the back seat and stared at the sign. Then they stared at each other.

It was nightfall by the time they got back to the house. Amber's dad made pizza while her mom worked on the computer.

After dinner, David went to his room and closed the door. The girls settled down in Amber's bedroom. Kelly looked through all of Amber's toys and books. They talked a little, then decided to go to sleep.

As they lay in the darkened bedroom, Kelly finally spoke.

"Amber, this is just about the creepiest stuff I've ever seen," she said. "I've always heard about the ghost out here, but I wasn't sure I believed it. Do you think your *house* is really haunted?"

"I don't know what to believe," Amber said. "But I got those letters. And I saw that picture of Helen McAfee on Mom's computer. And there was that message today at the school."

"What do you suppose it meant?" Kelly asked.

A cool breeze blew in through Amber's big window. Amber heard the soft chirping of crickets outside. She looked over and saw a full moon outside.

Then she heard the music.

It was the piano again. The music floated up the hill from Old Miss McAfee's house. This time it was some kind of classical piece, maybe Beethoven or Bach. It sounded soft, even kind of soothing.

"Does she play every night?" Kelly asked.

"Seems like it," Amber said.

The tune changed. It was that song again. The one Amber had heard in the car. The one the girls had heard on their ride down by Old Miss McAfee's garden.

"Come to me. Come to me, oh beautiful one."

Kelly started crying.

"I'm scared, Amber. I want to go home."

Amber climbed out of bed and walked to the window. She stared down into the moonlit yard.

And someone stared back up at her.

Chapter Thirty-Three

It was David.

He was standing in the yard all alone. He put his hand over his mouth, signaling Amber to be quiet. He waved for her to come down.

"Come on, Kelly," Amber said, stepping into her sandals. "David's down there. He wants to show us something."

"I'm not going out there, Amber," Kelly whimpered. "I'm scared. I want to go home."

"All right," Amber said. "You can stay here. But I'm going down to check it out."

Amber tiptoed down the stairs and sneaked past the room where her mom was still working. She went out the back door and closed it quietly.

David was still in the yard. He put his hand on her shoulder and pointed to the light in Old Miss McAfee's window.

"Look," he said.

Amber squinted. At first she did not see anything. The piano music had stopped. The wind began to blow a little harder.

Then she saw Old Miss McAfee standing in her yard. Her white hair blew wildly in the wind. She carried an old purse and walked toward an old garage behind her house.

David started walking down the hill.

"What do you think you're doing?" Amber asked, racing to catch up.

"Sssssh," he whispered sharply. "I'm going to see what she's up to."

The kids walked down through the dark woods to the house.

They heard a car engine start. It popped and roared, startling them. They were down on the old dirt trail, close to the spot where Old Miss McAfee had grabbed Amber.

"Duck down!" David said.

A set of headlights pulled out of the garage and headed towards them. They belonged to an ancient pickup truck, and Old Miss McAfee was behind the wheel. She drove slowly past Amber and David, who were hiding in the bushes.

"Thank goodness," David said. "She didn't see us."

Suddenly, they heard a loud *BLAM*. The old truck had backfired, and stalled.

Rrrrrrrrr. Rrrrrrrr. Rrrrrrr.

Old Miss McAfee was turning the key, trying to get it started again. David grabbed Amber's hand and tugged on it.

"Let's go see," he said, hopping up from their hiding spot.

Amber was terrified, but she followed her brother.

He crawled along the ground on his hands and knees, right up to the back of the truck.

To Amber's shock, he hopped onto the back! He motioned for her to join him. She froze, wide-eyed, and shook her head.

The truck started up again.

Screwing up all her courage, Amber hopped onto the back. The truck took off and turned onto the main road. Amber could tell that Old Miss McAfee had turned right.

She was heading for the river.

Chapter Thirty-Four

The old truck popped and jerked.

David and Amber lay down in the back. Apparently Old Miss McAfee had not noticed them. She drove very slowly. The truck weaved back and forth. Amber was afraid it was going to run off the road.

Guess she hasn't driven in a long time, Amber thought to herself.

She lay next to David, keeping as still as possible. She looked up at the big yellow moon, and watched the tree limbs pass overhead. David reached over and held her hand.

The truck rounded the bend, and headed down a hill. All of a sudden, Amber heard the sound of rushing water.

They were going over the old bridge!

The old planks popped and creaked as the truck drove over them. Amber looked back and saw the giant oak tree — the one her family had nearly hit the night they moved to Jackson.

An old rope hung from one of the branches. It had been broken, and it whipped wildly in the wind.

The truck turned sharply to the left, headed down a steep gravel road, and began rolling slowly through the woods.

David stared at Amber. She smelled smoke.

Then she heard a dog bark.

Chapter Thirty-Five

Slam!

The truck had stopped. It shook as Old Miss McAfee slammed the door. The kids heard her walking away.

After a few minutes, David peeked over the side of the truck bed.

"Look!" he whispered.

Amber sat up. They were parked in front of an old log cabin. It was very small, and pieces of the roof had caved in. The cabin was hidden by trees and vines. Tied to a rope in the yard, Amber and David saw the pit bulldog.

It was not barking any longer. Old Miss McAfee was nowhere in sight.

A faint light came from under the door of the place. Then the kids heard two voices shouting inside. The voices were muffled. Amber and David could not make out what the people were saying.

"I'm going to get closer," David said.

He hopped out of the truck and walked slowly up to the old cabin.

Amber was terrified. She did not want to be here. She certainly did not want to go any closer to this creepy place.

But she did not want to be left alone either, so she followed David.

They stopped in front of the rotting door. David pressed his ear to the wood. Amber did too.

They heard two voices. One belonged to a woman — Old Miss McAfee. The other belonged to a man. They were shouting at each other.

"You did this! You did this to me!" the man yelled. "What do you think you're doing? Are you trying to scare me or something? Why don't you just leave me alone!"

"I didn't do anything to you," Old Miss McAfee yelled back. "Look! I got one too!"

The pit bull began to growl. It stared at the kids huddled in front of the door, then began barking wildly.

With a jerk, someone threw open the door.

Chapter Thirty-Six

Amber and David stared into the face of a wild man.

His eyes were wide with rage. His hair was tousled. His clothes were dirty. He smelled bad.

The air in the whole place stank. The inside of the cabin was a mess. There was very little furniture. An old cot stood in one corner of the room. Empty soup cans and potato chip bags were piled on the floor.

Old Miss McAfee stood in the corner.

"Who are you?" the man screamed at the kids. "What are you doing here?"

Before either could answer, the man grabbed David by the neck and pulled him into the room. Then he reached for Amber.

The kids found themselves huddled on the floor. The wild man stood on one side of them. Old

Miss McAfee stood on the other.

"Don't hurt them!" she cried. "They're my grand-niece and grand-nephew. They're Carol's kids. She's just moved her family into the old house."

Amber and David stared in silence.

"You kids shouldn't be snooping around here," the man said in a low, mean voice. "You should mind your own business."

Then Amber spotted it. The wild man was holding a piece of paper. It was a faded, blue letter.

It looked just like the one she had gotten in the mail.

"I know what that is!" Amber blurted out. "It's a letter. And it's from Helen McAfee, isn't it?"

The wild man glared at her. He thrust the letter in front of her face.

"That's it, isn't it?" he said. "You kids are playing tricks on us, aren't you? Well, I'll show you what happens to kids who play tricks."

"No! No, Jim!" Old Miss McAfee cried out. "I got one too. And I don't see how these kids could have done it. It was in Helen's handwriting."

David grabbed Amber's hand and jumped up. He started to run out the door, but bumped into a table. An old record player sat on it, like one of those old phonographs the kids had seen in museums.

As David jumped back, a piece of metal with a needle on the end of it dropped down with a plunk and landed on an old record.

A scratchy tune began to play. A woman's voice sang sweetly.

"Come to me, come to me, my beautiful one. I am coming to you."

A faint ball of light began to materialize in the middle of the room. Amber could make out the shape of a woman. She was young. And very pretty.

And she had a white flower in her hair.

Chapter Thirty-Seven

The room was deadly quiet except for the soft sound of the music. Then Old Miss McAfee began to cry.

"Helen! Oh, Helen!" she sobbed. "It *is* you!"

The ghost looked over at her sister and smiled. Then she spoke.

"Amber, David," she said. "Don't be afraid. No one is going to hurt you. I've brought you all here for a reason."

Amber could not believe what was happening. Her heart pounded, and her throat felt so tight she had trouble breathing. David stared at the ghost with his mouth open.

"Something terrible has happened. Something more terrible than my death," the ghost continued. "Hannah, you stopped living the night I died. You know you had nothing to do with it. It was an accident. Jim, you've lied to everyone all these years. You let Hannah take the blame. It's time for it to stop."

The wild man began to cry.

"I'm sorry! I'm so sorry, Helen!" he wept. "I didn't mean for it to happen. You were angry and upset after the talent show. When I asked you to meet me out here by the tree, I didn't know what had happened. You thought I was seeing Hannah. You were hysterical. I was only trying to grab you to calm you down. I didn't mean to push you in the river!"

Amber and David stared in shock. The ghost spoke again.

"Jim, I know it was an accident. But you should have come forward and told what happened. You didn't. And my sister has had to live her whole life in shame and sadness. It's *your* fault. *You* need to make it right."

The ghost of Helen McAfee began to float across the room. It reached down and turned off the record player. Then it traveled in the air and stopped over Amber and David's heads.

"You children are my family," it said. "You need to help heal her. You've put me at peace."

The ghost floated over to Old Miss McAfee. They stared into one another's eyes, and looked very much alike. But one was old. The other was still a young girl.

The ghost paused over her sister, then leaned down and kissed her.

"I'm sorry," it said. "I love you. Be at peace."

In an instant, it was gone.

Amber heard the sound of breaking glass.

Chapter Thirty-Eight

The wild man — Jim — started smashing everything in the cabin.

He grabbed an iron poker from the side of the fireplace. He pounded the record player to pieces.

Then he turned toward Old Miss McAfee, and raised the poker over his head, ready to smash it down on her.

David jumped up and grabbed the poker. He and Jim wrestled wildly as Jim continued to flail with the poker.

Amber heard the sound of a siren. Car doors slammed. She heard footsteps running up to the cabin.

The door flew open. Sheriff Johnson burst in, pointing a gun.

"Stop right now!" he shouted. "Put down that poker."

Jim stared at the sheriff for what seemed like

114

several minutes. Then he hung his greasy head down, and let the poker drop to the floor.

Amber heard another car. Her mom, dad and Kelly rushed into the cabin.

"Oh, my gosh!" Amber's mom cried, running over to her son and daughter. "Are you all right? Are you all right?"

Amber started crying. David started shaking badly.

"I think we'd all better calm down and figure out what's going on here," Sheriff Johnson said. "Miss McAfee, can you tell us what happened?"

Old Miss McAfee was still crying. She walked over to a wooden stool and sat down. She didn't say a word.

David finally spoke.

"Mom, Dad, Sheriff Johnson," he said. "This is the man who killed Helen McAfee."

As the grown-ups stared in disbelief, David told them the whole story. Kelly stood by her dad, her eyes wide open as she listened.

Sheriff Johnson was quiet for a very long time.

"Jim. Is it true?" he asked, putting his gun back in his holster.

The wild man nodded his head.

"I'm not really sure what happened here to-night," Sheriff Johnson said. "I can't say that I believe that stuff about the ghost. But I do know that two kids were out in the night where they weren't supposed to be. David, Amber — your parents were worried sick about you."

Kelly piped up.

"I called Daddy to come take me home," she said. "But then we couldn't find you. I told them I had seen you two out the window going down to Old Miss McAfee's. Then I saw her truck head down here. So when Daddy got to the house, we figured that's where you must be."

"And a good thing, too," Amber's dad said. He sounded frightened and worried. "Sheriff Johnson, what are you going to do?"

"It doesn't look like anyone was hurt here," the sheriff said slowly, as if he were thinking out loud. "And I'm not sure we can do anything about some-thing that happened fifty years ago. And Helen McAfee's death was officially ruled an accident. Let's just leave it at that.

"But Jim," the sheriff continued. "I don't want to ever see you around these children again. Or near Miss McAfee. You seem to like keeping to yourself.

Keep it that way."

Amber and David walked out to the Honda. Their dad walked with them, an arm around each of them. Their mom went over to Miss McAfee and hugged her tightly.

"Why don't we get you home now," she said softly. "And let's get to know each other. I believe your story. It happened long ago. It's time to get on with your life now."

Carol walked Miss McAfee out to the truck. Kelly hopped in the patrol car with her dad, and waved good-bye to Amber.

Jim sat alone in the cabin, holding his head in his hands.

As the Ellistons drove home, Amber turned to look back at the big oak tree. Floating just underneath the branches, she saw the ghost one last time. It smiled at her.

Then Helen McAfee blew Amber a kiss.

Chapter Thirty-Nine

Everyone in the Elliston household slept late the next morning. By the time Amber made it downstairs to the kitchen, she noticed there was an extra plate on the breakfast table. Her dad sat down to eat. So did David and her mom.

Then in walked an old woman who looked kind of familiar, yet somehow different. Her white hair was tied in a neat bun. She wore a new dress, and smelled of perfume.

Oh my gosh! Amber realized. It's Old Miss McAfee!

But Amber's great aunt didn't look like a witch anymore. She was very pretty for an old woman. She smiled broadly and carried a pot of flowers.

"Here, Amber," she said. "These are for you."

She patted Amber on the head.

The family ate breakfast. Amber's dad dashed off to work. David went out in the back yard to shoot baskets.

"Amber," her mom said. "We all went through a horrible experience last night. But I've had a long talk with your great-aunt Hannah this morning. I think you've helped her a lot."

Then Miss McAfee spoke.

"I've lived my whole life alone, bitter and afraid," she said. "I didn't mean to scare you that day when you were down near my garden. But you looked so much like my sister when she was a little girl, I wanted to talk to you. I think maybe your coming here caused all these things to happen. I know some of them were very scary. I can't really explain it myself. But I've learned something very valuable. Love is important. And people are important. I want to get them back into my life."

Amber's mother spoke up.

"Honey, your great-aunt Hannah wants to give you piano lessons. Would you be interested?"

Amber had always wanted to play the piano. But she wasn't sure about going back down into Old Miss McAfee's house.

Her great-aunt sensed her fear.

"Come. Come with me," she said. "I think you're going to be surprised."

Chapter Forty

Amber got up from the table and followed Miss McAfee down the hill to her small, frame house.

It didn't look so spooky in the daytime. Someone had put big pots of fresh flowers all over the rickety front porch.

They went inside. The downstairs was just one big room. A beautiful old grand piano sat right in the middle.

Miss McAfee took her place on the piano bench, and motioned for Amber to sit next to her. The old woman pulled out some sheet music.

"This is a good one for us to start on," she said. "And a good way for us to get to know each other too."

As Miss McAfee began playing the simple tune, Amber looked around the room. Old family pictures covered the walls. There was a man in a soldier's uniform. A woman who looked like she might have lived during the Civil War. A family posed on a front porch. Amber recognized it as the house she now lived in.

Her eyes traveled to a neat round table standing next to the piano. It was covered with a beautiful, white embroidered cloth. An old picture in a gold frame stood on top of it.

It was a photograph of two young girls, sitting side by side. They both wore white party dresses. They both had blond, curly hair.

And each wore a white flower in her hair.

Miss McAfee stopped playing the piano for a moment.

"Yes," she said. "That's me and Helen."

Amber gasped. Twins! They were identical twins!

As Miss McAfee put her hands back on the keyboards and began the tune again, Amber took one long last look at the picture. She wasn't sure, but she could have sworn the girl who was Helen blinked her eyes and smiled.

Under the piano music, Amber heard a voice whispering faintly.

"Thank you," it whispered. *"Thank you."*

BE SURE TO READ THESE OTHER COLD, CLAMMY SHIVERS BOOKS.

THE CURSE OF THE NEW KID

LUCAS LYTLE IS USED TO BEING THE NEW KID IN SCHOOL. HE'S TWELVE YEARS OLD – AND HE'S ALREADY BEEN IN EIGHT DIFFERENT SCHOOLS. WHEN EVERYBODY FROM THE SCHOOL BULLIES TO THE CLASS NERDS PICK ON HIM, HE FEELS LIKE HE IS CURSED. BUT THEN STRANGE AND HORRIBLE THINGS START TO HAPPEN TO HIS ENEMIES. AT FIRST LUCAS IS CONFUSED BY WHAT IS HAPPENING. BUT THEN HE STARTS TO ENJOY IT – UNTIL IT BECOMES TOO FRIGHTENING FOR HIM TO HANDLE.

LET, LET, LET
THE
MAILMAN
GIVE YOU COLD, CLAMMY
SHIVERS! SHIVERS!
SHIVERS!!!

A Frightening Offer: Buy the first
Shivers book at $3.99 and pick each
additional book for only $1.99. Please include $2.00 for
shipping and handling.
Canadian orders: Please add $1.00 per book.

___ #1 The Enchanted Attic
___ #2 A Ghastly Shade of Green
___ #3 The Ghost Writer
___ #4 The Animal Rebellion
___ #5 The Locked Room
___ #6 The Haunting House
___ #7 The Awful Apple Orchard

___ #8 Terror on Troll Mountain
___ #9 The Mystic's Spell
___ #10 The Curse of the New
    Kid
___ #11 Guess Who's Coming
    For Dinner?
___ #12 The Secret of Fern
    Island

I'm scared, but please send me the books checked above.

$_____ is enclosed.

Name_____

Address _____

City_____ State_____ Zip _____

**Payment only in U.S. Funds. Please no cash or C.O.D.s.
Send to: Paradise Press, 8551 Sunrise Blvd. #302,
Plantation, FL 33322.**